For my mothers and sister,
Karen, Amy and Amee
Thank you for who you are
- J.M.W.

First hardback edition 2020

Book design by Travis A. Thompson

ISBN 978-0-578-72138-5 (hardback)
ISBN 978-0-578-72140-8 (ebook)

www.arewethatdifferent.net

Are We That Different?

Written by: Jasmine Wooten

Illustrated by: Travis A. Thompson

I have blue eyes.
You have brown.
Mine are more square
and yours more round.

Are we that different?
Not that much...

I like skating.
You like double dutch.

My hair is long.
Yours is kind of short.

I laugh with a giggle
and you with a snort!

I like cream and
you like honey.
Are we that different?
Nahhhh!

We both love ice cream.
Yummy!

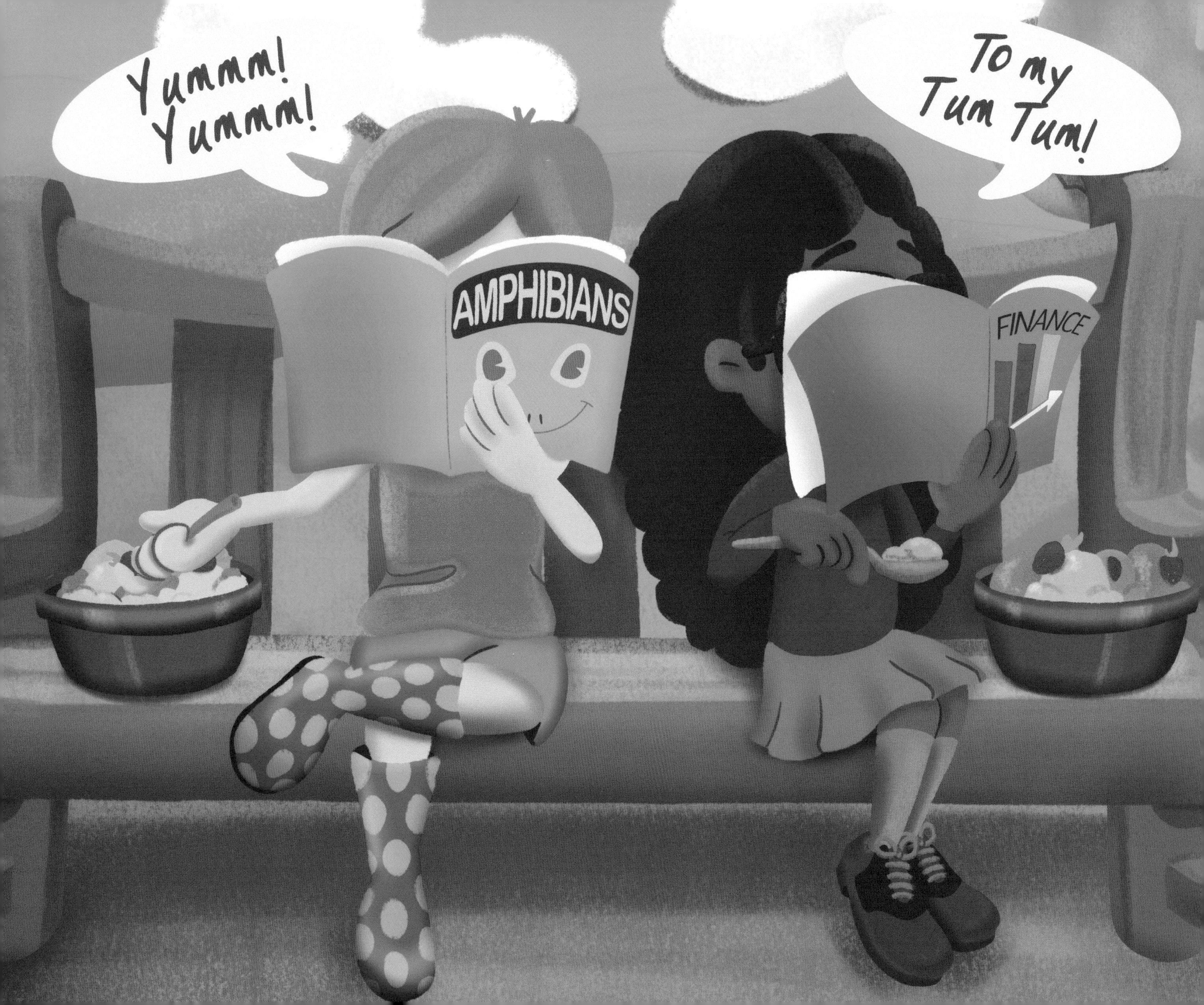
Yummm! Yummm!
To my Tum Tum!
AMPHIBIANS
FINANCE

I'm kind of small.
You're about...there.

I sleep with a night light.
You still sleep with Offie
your teddy bear.

Are we best friends?
I surely think so.

Are we that different?
I would say NO!

Jasmine Wooten writes inspirational and self affirming children's books for diverse audiences. Her passion for encouraging children to be their best selves is a continuous goal. Hailing from Detroit, Michigan, Jasmine remains steadfast in her quest to provide a place in the hearts of children where anything is possible.

CPSIA information can be obtained at www.ICGtesting.com
Printed in the USA
BVIW120802111120
592858BV00020B/21